Also by Pippa Funnell

Tilly's Horse, Magic

Team Training

Pippa Funnell

Orion
Children's Books

First published in Great Britain in 2014
by Orion Children's Books
a division of the Orion Publishing Group Ltd
Orion House
5 Upper St Martin's Lane
London WC2H 9EA
An Hachette Livre UK Company

3 5 7 9 8 6 4 2

A catalogue record for this book is
available from the British Library.

ISBN 978 1 4440 1200 2

Printed and bound by CPI Group (UK) Ltd, Croydon, CR0 4YY

www.orionbooks.co.uk

To Gill Watson
for her devoted work over many years
as team trainer for the juniors and young riders

Chapter One

Tilly Redbrow knew that not everyone's dreams came true. Some people didn't have dreams at all. They had no idea what they wanted to do with their future, where they'd like to go, or who they'd go there with. Not Tilly. She'd known since she was little that she wanted to work with horses. And from the moment she'd first sat in the saddle, she'd known she wanted to be a true champion. But, above all, she'd known that the horse she wanted to win with was her beloved grey, Magic Spirit. She couldn't believe that today she was a step closer to that dream coming true. She was on her way to Junior Squad training.

She leaned across the passenger seat of Mrs Ashton-Smith's horsebox and peered at the sat nav.

'It's not far now,' she said, checking the distance it showed they still had to travel.

'Just a few miles,' said Mrs Ashton-Smith. 'Look out for a turning on the left. What's the name of the farm again?'

'Hancocks,' said Tilly proudly. 'Hancocks Farm and Event Yard.'

She sat back, twiddled her horsehair bracelets, and watched as they sped past woods and fields, keen to catch her first glimpse of the yard. She was thrilled that she was about to spend a week living and training with Livvy James, an international event rider she'd always admired. When she was younger, she'd watched her on television, unable to tear herself away as Livvy had simply sailed over the most terrifying-looking obstacles Tilly had ever seen at the Badminton and Burghley Horse

Trials. Livvy was known for being brilliant in all three phases: dressage, show jumping and cross country. Tilly had posters of her all over her bedroom walls – Livvy and her amazing thoroughbred, Evening Star. The biggest poster still hung above her bed, an image of Evening Star, a rich dark chestnut with a white blaze, staring out with big bold eyes. Tilly had gazed at that image a thousand times, had dreamed of what it would be like to ride a horse that incredible.

That was before she'd met Magic though. Things had changed. Her success riding Magic, rising through the area competitions, then impressing at the Pony Club championships, had earned her a place on the Junior Squad. The week-long training with Livvy was her first squad requirement. And as if that wasn't brilliant enough, Tilly had found out that her brother, Brook, also a talented rider, would be joining them too, with his wonderful horse, Solo.

Brook gave Tilly a nudge.

'Do you think Livvy James will be there to meet us in person?'

'I hope so,' said Tilly. 'I'm worried I'll be stupidly star-struck though. What if I get flustered or go bright red every time I see her . . .'

Brook smiled. 'I wouldn't worry. You'll get used to being around her. I bet she's really nice. I've heard her talk on the radio and she sounds friendly. Anyway, I'm not sure it's Livvy James you need to worry about—'

Tilly pulled a face. She knew exactly who Brook was referring to. Kya Mackenzie. The name flashed through her mind. Even though Tilly and Kya were both members of the squad and had been team mates at the Pony Club championships, they were also rivals. Their worst fall-out had cost them a win at the championships and, although they'd made up, Tilly felt wary of Kya. She couldn't forget that she'd betrayed her trust, spreading gossip about Tilly being too poor to afford a horse like Magic, about Magic being a 'stolen' ride – and if there was one thing Tilly was sensitive about, it was Magic. True, he wasn't officially hers, but it wasn't because she'd stolen him. It was because she'd *rescued* him.

Tilly stared out of the window, and suddenly felt the anxiety rise in her chest. She hated the thought that Magic's real owner, the cruel person who'd apparently abandoned him on a dangerous roadside, could one day come marching into the yard at Silver Shoe Farm and claim him. It kept her awake at night, the worry that Magic could be taken from her, that there'd be nothing she could do about it. The thought was too upsetting. Especially on such an exciting day. Quickly, she looked for distraction.

'Look,' said Brook. 'Did you see that?'

'What?'

'A sign with a horse logo.'

Tilly turned. There it was, an elegant wooden board, saying 'Hancocks Farm and Event Yard' above a small silhouette of a galloping horse. Brook's mum turned the wheel of the horsebox and skilfully manoeuvred the vehicle into the lane.

At first, all Tilly could see were hedgerows. The lane seemed to go on forever, winding and curving, like a road to nowhere. Then, through a gap in the foliage she spotted a huge sunlit stretch of grass and, beyond it, an array of red brick barns and stables. It was the only dwelling in the entire valley, surrounded on all sides by woods and hills. There were horses everywhere, all different colours, but all with quality, grazing in the fields. The familiar scent of hay and manure wafted through the open window. She breathed it in and smiled.

'I promise I won't worry about Kya Mackenzie,' she said, giving Brook a nod. 'I'm not going to let *anything* spoil this week.'

'Good for you, sis,' said Brook. 'Hey, I think we're the first to get here.'

Brook's mum parked and the three of them hopped out of the cab.

'Such a long drive,' said Tilly, yawning

and stretching. 'I hope Magic and Solo are okay.'

She glanced around the yard. She desperately wanted to see Livvy James, but at the same time, the prospect filled her with nerves. Just as she was looking at the farmhouse, the back door swung open. A young man waved.

'Hey! You're juniors that have come for training, right? Welcome to Hancocks!'

'Hi,' said Brook. 'Thanks. I'm Brook Ashton-Smith and this is my sister, Tilly Redbrow. And this is my mum. She's just dropping us off.'

Brook's mum beamed with pride. The man marched over and shook their hands.

'My name's Nick,' he said. 'You'll be seeing a lot of me this week. I'm Livvy's right-hand man. I manage the yard for her.'

Tilly wanted to ask him where Livvy was, but didn't dare.

'You've had quite a journey, I expect,' he said. 'Let's get your horses settled. I'll get a couple of our girls to help you. Then you can relax while you wait for the others.'

Brook and Tilly went round to the back of the lorry, let the ramp down and climbed into the back. Magic and Solo both whickered with delight on hearing their familiar voices.

'I think they're looking forward to some fresh air,' said Tilly.

Brook led Solo down the ramp, while Tilly attended to Magic. She opened his partition and gave him a huge hug.

'Hello, boy. Haven't you been patient? But guess what? We're here!'

Magic pricked his ears and whinnied. She untied his rope, gave him a reassuring pat, then led him down the ramp. As soon as he got to the bottom, however, one of Nick's stable hands, a young girl with spiky red hair, stepped forward to introduce herself. Maybe it was the spiky hair or simply the fact that she was unfamiliar, but Magic immediately threw up his head and flattened his ears.

'Whoa!' said Tilly. 'It's okay, boy!'

Magic snorted alarmingly. The red-haired girl moved away, but his mood continued.

'Do you need a hand?' said Nick. 'Perhaps he'll be happier once he's stabled?'

He offered to take him from Tilly.

'Best not to,' she said. 'He can be a bit funny with people he doesn't know. Don't worry, I'll get him calm.'

She held Magic, touched his face, got him to look at her rather than worry about the strange people and buildings around him, then whispered in a firm, low voice.

'Good boy. That's it, good boy, Magic. You know I'm here. So behave yourself.'

Eventually, he lowered his head and settled down.

'Wow!' said Nick. 'Nice work. You've got a hypnotic touch, Tilly.'

'Thanks,' she replied.

For the next half hour, she walked Magic around and gave him a pick of grass, figuring it was the best way to get him used to the new environment. She led him past the stable blocks and around the big barns, then alongside the indoor and outdoor arenas. Everything was immaculate. It was the tidiest yard she'd ever seen. It was pretty too. The paths were lined with terracotta planters full of colourful busy lizzies. The grass pastures were lush and the sand school was perfectly harrowed and the corners all hand-raked. Grooms and horses came and went, looking busy and purposeful.

Eventually, Tilly came to a fence and what looked like the end of Livvy James' land. After lingering for a while, she realised it was time to head back. Brook would be wondering where she and Magic had got to, and Magic needed to be stabled. She tugged on his lead rope and was about to walk away, when she heard the clip-clopping of hooves. There, beyond the fence, oblivious to the fact that anyone might be watching, Livvy James emerged over the crest of the hill, against a blazing blue sky, in the saddle of an all too familiar horse – the magnificent Evening Star.

Tilly stopped in her tracks. Magic also stood to attention, as though he knew what this moment meant to her. All Tilly could think was that there, in front of her – breathing, living, real – were the horse and rider who were her inspiration. And now, *now* they were riding towards her.

Chapter Two

'Hi.'

Tilly blinked, finding it impossible to hide her awe. She gazed at Livvy's shining black riding boots, her spotless breeches. She was mesmerised by the way she sat in the saddle, with a perfect position.

'I – I'm Tilly Redbrow,' she said, open-mouthed. 'I'm part of the Junior Squad. I'm here for our training week.'

Livvy James smiled.

'Yes, of course. We've been expecting you.'

Tilly couldn't stop staring at Evening Star, his

shining chestnut coat and white blaze. He had a wise face, but he looked keen and alert.

'He's even better in real life than he is in the posters!'

'Huh?'

'Evening Star.'

'Oh, yes.' Livvy leaned forward and gave the horse a pat. 'Still going strong. He doesn't compete any more, but I'll never give him up. He won me my first ever four-star three-day event.'

'Can I stroke him?' asked Tilly, mesmerised.

'Sure.'

Tilly ran her hand down Evening Star's silky nose, felt the warmth of his breath, the tickly hairs around his nostrils.

'Hello, beautiful,' she whispered. 'It's an honour to meet you.'

'And who is *this*?' said Livvy, nodding at Magic.

'This is Magic Spirit.'

Tilly explained how he'd been a bit tense after being cooped up in the horsebox, so she'd been walking him round the yard to get him used to the new surroundings.

'I was just about to take him back to the stables.'

'Well, that's where I'm heading too,' said Livvy. 'Evening Star has had his exercise for the day. Also, I guess the rest of the squad are due to arrive.'

'I'm sorry,' said Tilly. 'We got here early.'

'That's fine by me,' said Livvy. 'In a busy yard like Hancocks, efficiency is always appreciated. Let's walk together.'

Tilly and Livvy led their horses up the track, past the barns and the sand school. Every step of the way, Tilly had to pinch herself. She felt a bit silly because she was too awestruck to think of anything sensible to say, but luckily Livvy was distracted. As soon as they reached the main yard, she was swamped by stable hands. There were questions about which horses needed exercising and clipping, which ones needed to be prepared for competition, which ones were having their shoes replaced. Livvy had answers for everyone. She was clear, focused and no-nonsense. Meanwhile, Evening Star stood patiently beside her, like a loyal guardian.

When all the questions had been dealt with, Livvy showed Tilly where Magic could be stabled. She even helped fetch a water bucket and haynet.

'Wow,' Tilly whispered to Magic. 'It's not every day you get looked after by a legend.'

Magic just snorted and shoved his nose in the hay.

'It looks like the rest of your squad are here,' said Livvy. 'I am ready for a cup of tea, so let's go and meet them in the kitchen. By the way, I'm terrible with names, so you'll have to remind me who they all are.'

Then she glanced at Tilly and smiled.

'But I'll definitely remember your name. Tilly, right?'

Together, Tilly and Livvy walked through the farmhouse door, into the kitchen. The entire Junior Squad, including Brook, handsome Harry Grey, and Tilly's Pony Club championship team mates, Ben, Kya and Anna, were all sitting round the large pine kitchen table. However, the first person to notice her entrance was Kya. She was sitting at the head of the table, looking perfect in a navy-blue polo shirt, with not a strand of her ice-blonde hair out of place. When she saw that Tilly was standing beside Livvy James – *the* Livvy James – she sucked in her cheeks and frowned slightly.

Livvy gave them a warm greeting and invited Tilly to sit beside her. Tilly was glad to have Brook on the other side, to shield her from Kya's glare. She looked around the table and said hi to her friends.

'Hey, Tilly,' said Ben. 'We were wondering where you'd got to.'

'Looks like you've already settled in,' said Anna, with a friendly wink.

'All right, Tilly,' said Harry Grey, as he caught Tilly's eye.

Immediately, Tilly could feel the heat rise in her cheeks. What was it about Harry? Horses were her life. She didn't have time for boys – not like her friends at school, who were mad about boys. For Tilly, it was all about riding, Pony Club and eventing. But then there was Harry . . .

'How's Magic?' he asked. 'Brook said he was a bit unsettled after the journey.'

'He's fine now, thanks,' said Tilly.

Livvy clapped her hands.

'I just want to welcome you to your first ever Junior Squad training week,' she said. 'I gather you've met my head lad, Nick.'

Nick poked his head out of the next-door office and waved.

'Don't mind me,' he said. 'I'm just sorting out yet another horse transportation crisis, then I'll introduce myself properly.'

'Are you guys always this busy?' said Brook.

'Twenty-four seven,' said Livvy. 'We're one of the busiest event yards in the country, so it never stops – but don't worry, you'll soon get used to the pace. And if you don't,' she paused and looked at each of them in turn, 'then you're probably not cut out for eventing at the top level.'

Although Livvy had a friendly manner, Tilly could tell that she also meant business. Her standards were clearly high, so it was up to them to prove themselves to her.

'If you think you've come to Hancocks Farm for a riding holiday,' she continued, 'then think again. You're going to work harder than you've ever worked in your lives. From dawn until dusk, you'll be helping my team and they'll be helping you. You'll see first-hand how we run the yard, and how our event horses are managed, cared for and trained. Take note of the care and attention every one of our horses is given. Watch carefully how we train them and please don't be afraid to ask any of us questions, whether it's how we do things or if you need anything. We're here to help, but you must appreciate we have an awful lot to get through in a day. It's simple. The more you get involved and the more attention you pay, the more you'll learn. Just so you know, there *will* be time for you to practise and improve your own riding skills. I, personally, want to oversee some sessions with you, but this isn't a jolly. It's serious now, a once-in-a-lifetime opportunity to start preparing for a future in eventing. Any questions?'

Tilly's mind began to race. She had so many. She didn't know where to start. Her arm shot up. Livvy smiled at her.

'How many horses do you have here?'

'We have stable room for fifty, but currently, we're looking after forty-five. We've recently started a breeding programme, so we've got several young horses that we're bringing on. We hope that, one day, there'll be a few champions among them.'

Tilly's hand went up again.

'How often do you compete?'

'Every weekend – at least, that's what it feels like sometimes. We were in Germany last weekend. Italy before that.'

'And how many staff do you have?'

'Oh, ten and a couple of part-time helpers.'

Tilly was about to ask another question, when she noticed Kya roll her eyes. Self-consciously, she lowered her hand and shrank into her seat. Brook asked a question about cross country, but instead of listening to Livvy's answer, Tilly began to feel annoyed. Why did Kya have to be so mean? She could hear her whispering to Harry.

'Who exactly does Tilly think she is? Listen to her. She won't leave Livvy alone. It's like she's some kind of psycho super-fan.'

Tilly was glad to see that Harry just shrugged Kya's comment off, but it still hurt. After the disastrous argument at the Pony Club championships, the girls had made a promise to support each other, but it didn't seem as though Kya was sticking to it. Tilly did her best to remember the conversation she'd had with Brook on the way over, about how she wasn't going to let Kya spoil her week at Hancocks. Easier said than done.

Eventually the conversation came round to Livvy's career and all the competitions she'd won. She told them how she had left school at sixteen and served a six-year apprenticeship with an amazing lady who taught her all she knew. In the first couple of years all the horses she rode were the real youngsters because she was the only person in the yard brave enough to and she had incredible stick-ability. When the three-year-olds bucked and turned themselves inside out, she had an uncanny knack of staying on them. She explained that, without knowing it, these youngsters had taught her more about horsemanship than any lesson would. She talked briefly about some of her major wins, but kept on coming back to 'it was thanks to this horse or that trainer' or 'it was that owner who made it possible'.

She was very cleverly giving the group their first lesson, and she wanted them to realise that to be a top rider it was not just about them. It was about a large team and that team included horses, owners, sponsors, trainers, grooms. The list went on and on, everyone playing a very important role. Tilly was relieved to discover that actually she wasn't the only star-struck member of the squad. The way they listened attentively, Anna, Ben and Harry were obviously fans too – but funnily enough Kya didn't have any smart remarks to make about *their* admiration.

Eventually, Livvy stood up.

'Right, well, if that's all the questions,' she said, 'then I'll get Nick to show you to your sleeping quarters, give you a chance to get some rest before the hard work begins. It's great to have you here. Please make yourselves at home. But remember, I'm looking for talent, graft and dedication. There'll be no special treatment or favouritism,' she glanced at each of them, 'so don't think you can win me over by flattering me. Just impress me with your commitment.'

With that, she smiled and left the kitchen.

Chapter Three

Early next morning, Tilly was lost in a lovely
dream about competing at the European
championships. She and Magic were just about
to cross the finish line, when the buzz of an
alarm clock woke her up. She opened her
eyes, took a moment to gather her wits, then
remembered she was in the little bedroom above
the farmhouse kitchen. In the single beds next
to her were Anna and Kya. They both groaned
and sat up.

'Uh. Is it morning already?' said Anna. 'Now
I remember why I wanted to give up eventing.'

'I'm glad you didn't,' said Tilly, remembering how, after problems with her mum, Anna had come close to quitting riding at competitions – luckily Tilly had managed to convince her not to. 'If you'd given up, you wouldn't get to spend the week with Livvy James.'

'True,' said Anna, yawning. 'But I *would* get lie-ins.'

Kya leaped out of bed and pulled on a T-shirt and a pair of designer jeans – much smarter than the ones Tilly used for yard work.

'Come on, Anna,' she said, tugging the duvet off her. 'Let's go to the bathroom and brush our teeth. Livvy and Nick said they want us in the yard by seven.'

Tilly noticed Kya didn't include her. It felt as if she was leaving her out deliberately.

'I'll come too,' she said, grabbing her wash-bag. 'After all, we're a team. We're on the same squad.'

Kya sniffed.

'But that doesn't mean we have to do everything together, does it? You know, we may have made up at the championships, Tilly, but I haven't forgotten that you ruined my cross country. And to be honest, I don't think it's something I will forget in a hurry.'

With that, she turned and marched off.

Tilly blinked.

'Ignore her,' whispered Anna. 'You know how she likes to get all huffy about stuff.'

Tilly sighed and nodded. She should have known her truce with Kya wouldn't last, but she was determined not to get caught up in her pettiness. She took a breath, looked in the mirror and started plaiting her hair.

It was a bright morning. As soon as the girls stepped outside, they felt properly refreshed. The yard was already busy. Livvy was working her second horse of the morning, having cantered one early. Horses had already been fed and the staff were hard at work, getting on with mucking out and haying. A couple of horses were being led out to a paddock while others that looked younger were coming in. The girls were greeted by the faces of their three horses, Magic, Bastion and Matinee, who bobbed their heads eagerly over the stable doors.

Magic looked much more settled than he had yesterday. Tilly was glad.

'Good morning,' she said, kissing his nose and rubbing his neck. 'Did you sleep well? It's time to get you fed and ready for the day. I wonder what we'll be doing.'

She led Magic outside, tied him up and gave him a small haynet. Then she borrowed mucking-out equipment from the red-headed groom she'd met the day before, quickly cleared the soiled bedding from Magic's stable floor and added a fresh bag of wood shavings. As she was filling Magic's water bucket, Nick came by.

'Good morning, Tilly. I'm pleased to see Magic seems to have calmed down. Once you're done here, you can come and help with the rest of the horses. We like to have all mucking out and tidying done by 9.00 a.m.'

'Sure,' said Tilly.

She gave Magic his water, and a quick cuddle, then joined the rest of the juniors in the tack room, where Nick was coordinating the day's work. She saw Brook and smiled, but there was no time to chat. They were each assigned a couple of horses and told to muck out and feed them. Tilly was given a young brown horse called Archie Boy and a steel-grey mare called Delilah Sweet.

She found Delilah Sweet straightaway – her stable was near Magic's. She was a quiet, good-natured mare, who stood patiently tied up while Tilly went back and forth to the muck-heap. Archie Boy, however, was a bit of a pest. He put his head up so high Tilly could hardly get his head collar on, then he kicked the bucket of water Tilly had filled for him. Worried that the other stable hands might think she wasn't in control, Tilly did her best to discipline him. She tried to reassure him, but all he did was stamp his feet and scream for his companion, who was having an early session in the school with Livvy. One of the stable hands nearby looked up.

'Don't worry,' he said. 'That's typical Archie Boy. He plays up for everyone. Don't take it personally. You're doing a good job there.'

'Thanks,' said Tilly, feeling happier.

When she finally finished with Archie Boy, she stretched and yawned, worn out by all the forking and sweeping. She saw Brook, Ben and Harry crossing the yard and ran to catch up with them. They looked as exhausted as she was. Ben glanced at his watch.

'Nearly 8.30 a.m. Hey, we've finished early! Nick will be pleased. I guess we must be extra-efficient.'

'Let's get some breakfast,' said Brook. 'I'm starving.'

'We've certainly earned it,' said Harry.

Just as they were nearing the farmhouse, however, Nick called them back.

'Where are you four off to?'

'Um, we've finished our horses, so we're going to get something to eat.'

'Who said anything about *finished*?' said Nick, a glint in his eye. 'There are twenty more to do yet. Come with me.'

He marched back to the tack room and pointed to a large whiteboard. All the horses' names were marked on a grid, with different coloured symbols to represent what they'd had done.

'If you're ever in doubt,' he explained, 'look at the board. This is where all the yard information is recorded. It'll tell you who's been mucked out, who hasn't, who's had exercise, who still needs exercise, and any other important stuff, such as special diets, medication and treatments. It's vital to keep track of activity in a busy yard like this, otherwise things get overlooked. And we don't want that. Right now, I can see that all these horses still need doing.'

He pointed to a row of names and blank squares.

'Back to work,' he said.

When, at last, every horse on Nick's white-board had been mucked out and the yard tidily swept, the juniors were allowed to head back to the farmhouse. As they opened the kitchen door, a welcoming smell greeted them, freshly cooked eggs and bacon. Livvy's housekeeper, Clare, ushered them to the table and grinned.

'Since it's your first day,' she said, 'Livvy suggested I spoil you with one of my fry-ups. Who's hungry?'

There was a sea of nods. Everyone tucked in, except for Kya, who said she was following a strict diet and had her own special organic food that she'd brought from home.

'That looks like something I'd feed Hunter,' said Ben, nodding at Kya's bowl of powdery cereal.

'My body is a temple,' she replied. 'So there's

no way I'm polluting it with all that greasy bacon fat.'

Clare pulled a face. Brook shook his head.

'This is delicious, thanks, Clare,' he said politely.

'Fuel!' said Ben, biting a sausage in half. 'Yard work is hard work!'

'It's amazing how many horses they have to manage here,' said Tilly, between mouthfuls. 'But we did it!'

She was tired, but also impressed by the tight organisation of Nick's stable routine. There was obviously a lot she could learn from working alongside someone as experienced as him. Kya didn't seem so convinced.

'It's tiresome,' she moaned. 'I've come here to enhance my talent in the saddle, not to be a stable yard *dogsbody*.'

Tilly caught Brook's eye. Brook smiled and gave a little shrug.

'Well, personally, *I'm* not above yard work,' he said. 'Even if it means getting my hands dirty.'

'So true,' said Livvy, who'd suddenly appeared in the doorway. 'The more hands-on a rider is with their horses – and that includes mucking out and grooming – the greater the bond between them. And a strong bond between a horse and rider means everything, especially during tough events. I have to admit that these days, I have so many to ride or I'm busy with sponsors or sorting out paperwork for competitions, but whenever I can, I handle and care for the horses myself. I'm *definitely* not above yard work.'

Tilly smiled and nodded, full of admiration for Livvy. Kya, meanwhile, scowled into her cereal bowl. Anna took a sip of orange juice and bravely asked Livvy if there was a chance they'd get to ride today. Livvy thought for a moment.

'Hm. Nick has plans for you this morning. I'm busy talking to my agent about a new sponsorship deal I've been offered, so Nick's going to be looking after you. There's a jumping course in the sand school that needs dismantling.

But hopefully, I'll have some time to spend with you later. I want to see each of you ride, so I can get a sense of your strengths and weaknesses. Right, back to work . . .'

Tilly sank into her seat. She couldn't help feeling a little disappointed that a ride with Livvy would have to wait until later, but she could see how hectic Livvy's schedule was. Horses to ride. Sponsorship deals. Media appearances. Entries to make. Competition training. Livvy never stopped – and yet she always put her horses first.

As they gathered at the gate of the sand school, Kya continued to grumble about being a dogsbody, but no one paid attention. Nick opened the gate for them.

'These cross poles were set up to help us bring on some of our young horses. We're hoping we can produce some to be top horses in the future. At this stage, we're trying to improve their technique over a fence, hence the cross poles. Livvy likes to get the basics right, before she asks her horses more challenging questions.'

Tilly looked across the array of poles. They reminded her of when she'd first learned to jump, back at Silver Shoe Farm, on a gentle pony called Rosie. She felt a surge of pride to think of that moment and realise how far she and Magic had come since.

'Tilly . . . *Tilly* . . .'

Brook gave her a nudge.

'Are you with us?'

'Uh, yes, I was just . . . just reminiscing.'

'Come on, Planet Pony . . . Nick wants us to take these jumps down then replace them with more challenging ones.'

'Okey-dokey,' said Tilly vaguely.

As she walked across the sand, she found herself lingering in her daydream, reliving the moment she first felt Rosie lift off the ground, the buzz, the thrill. When she finally looked up, she noticed Harry Grey had been watching her – not just watching, but *watching*. He smiled. She smiled. Then she blushed like crazy.

Chapter Four

In the afternoon, true to her word, Livvy met the juniors at the farmhouse and discussed the programme for the rest of the day.

'I have been pretty frantic this morning, I have a couple more horses to work, which you can all watch and then I want to see you guys ride, so have your horses ready for 3.30 p.m.'

'As it's the first time you will have ridden your horses since you arrived yesterday, I thought it would be a good idea to give them a canter and a short sharp blow, by that I mean open them up and gallop them, but only for a short distance. I can look at your positions as you're cantering and it will probably make the horses easier for you tomorrow when I have something a little bit different up my sleeve, but you'll have to wait to find out what.'

The Junior Squad watched in awe, mouths gaping wide in disbelief, as Livvy worked the freakish nine-year-old, Celtic Surprise, who was just stepping up to the top level. Livvy struggled to hide her excitement over the horse, feeling that he was one of the best young horses that she had ever produced. He'd won every major event he had competed in, his record was unheard of. He moved with such lightness that it looked as though he hardly touched the ground, as though he was floating.

Watching, Tilly now understood the meaning of a great partnership, horse and rider working in true harmony together. Even Ben falling off the fence next to the sand school and causing the others to burst into hysterical laughter didn't distract this magnificent creature.

'How will we ever be that good?' Tilly asked her mates.

'Work, work and more work. Dedication.' Livvy replied, overhearing the conversation.

The next horse they watched was a complete contrast, a very spooky five-year-old called Ship A' Hoy.

'He is aptly named, and is like a boat to ride,' said Livvy light-heartedly, explaining that the reason for the stiffness through his body was due to the fact that he was very long in his back, yet he had good movement and a huge, careful jump.

'With Ship, I am going by my gut instinct. With the correct work over several years I feel he will strengthen up and become a very good horse, but lots of patience will be needed along the way.'

Looking at her watch, Livvy reminded them of the time.

Even Kya was completely absorbed in

watching and listening to Livvy at work. Fascinated was an understatement, they could hardly tear themselves away.

'I could watch Livvy ride all day,' said Tilly.

'Come on, I feel inspired, let's tack up and get going,' Brook replied.

Tilly rushed to the tack room to collect Magic's saddle and bridle. She knew Harry was close behind. The tack room was the biggest they had ever seen, all oak-panelled. She had never seen so much kit: bridles hanging in immaculately neat rows along the full length of one of the walls, rows of saddles on another, in the corner was a smart sink set into an oak kitchen unit, different kinds of bits hung neatly on one section of wall, underneath rows of competition plaques that Livvy had collected from competitions all over the world.

Tilly lifted her saddle carefully from one of the racks.

'I love the smell of leather, don't you?' she said, filling the silence.

Harry smiled.

'Best smell in the world.'

He hooked his saddle over his arm and waited for her as she grabbed her martingale out of her metal tack trunk.

'It feels like such a privilege, doesn't it?' he said, as they walked out. 'I can't believe we're about to go up Livvy James' gallops and she is going to help us. I'd muck out a thousand horses for that opportunity.'

'Me too, said Tilly, managing not to blush this time.

Tilly had already brushed Magic earlier in the day. She put his numnah in place, then gently lifted the saddle onto his back and buckled up the girth, attaching the running martingale before she put the bridle on. She was slightly nervous about cantering with the others, knowing Magic would get strong, so as well as a martingale which would prevent him from getting his head too high, she decided to put him in a slightly stronger snaffle.

He seemed excited by the prospect of going out in a group. He shuffled anxiously to and fro, trying to sniff Brook's horse, Solo, and Ben's horse, Hedgehunter.

To everyone's surprise, Livvy reappeared, leading Evening Star.

'You don't expect me to be on my feet while you canter, it's a bit of a hike to my all-weather gallops,' Livvy explained. 'I could take the quad bike but I thought Evening Star would love to have a canter. Since he's retired he doesn't get to go up the gallops very often. He is well bred to race, so I am sure that was why he loved galloping more than any other kind of work.'

She mounted and checked her girth, tightening it slightly. The others followed.

'Before we set off, I want all of you to put your stirrups up three holes,' Livvy said.

'I've never ridden this short before,' exclaimed Kya. 'How can I possibly sit up tall with stirrups this short?'

'The reason I'm making you ride shorter,' said Livvy, 'is because you will find it easier to balance when you stand up off their backs as you canter, similar to how you should be when you gallop between cross country fences.'

'This is cool. I feel like a jockey,' Ben said, turning to the others.

'And NO RACING, BOYS,' warned Livvy, as she nudged Evening Star forward and out of the yard.

The horses all keenly bounced out of the yard, jig-jogging.

'I want you guys to be sensible and not get too close to each other,' Livvy said, as they made their way through a gate, turning down a muddy track, slippy from a short sharp shower earlier that morning. 'I don't want any of you, or your horses, getting kicked.'

Magic did his best to cope with the footing, affected by the mud because he was too excited to walk.

Kya looked over her shoulder.

'You okay, Tilly?' she said, loud enough for Livvy to hear. 'You're wobbling all over the place!'

Tilly clenched her jaw. 'We're fine,' she said quickly. 'We're just getting used to the mud.'

'Don't worry,' said Livvy. 'The track gets better ahead.'

Fifteen minutes later they arrived at the bottom of the gallops. The perfectly harrowed and rolled sand and wax surface started at the bottom of the valley and climbed gradually for nearly a kilometre, then more steeply for five hundred metres, before flattening out at the top. It was an excellent gallop for getting horses fit.

'I think it's best we go up in pairs. If you think the horses will canter alongside each other, great,' Livvy said. 'If not, put the stronger of the two in front. I'll set off first with Ben and Hedgehunter, then wait until we're halfway up before the next pair set off. No racing, just a nice steady canter, half the speed you would go if you were riding cross country.'

Before they set off, Livvy stood in her stirrups and demonstrated the position she wanted the juniors to work on as they went up the gallops.

'Even when you stand in your stirrups, think about your legs being on the girth and your hips being over your heels, remembering to work your horses up to the contact, with your hands nice and still.'

Livvy and Ben set off up the gallops while the others had been instructed to wait and patiently walk in the large square area at the bottom. Once at the top Livvy watched them coming up the gallops two by two. Some of the horses were a bit keen at the bottom, but when they got to the steeper part they had settled.

'Great job, you guys,' Livvy said enthusiastically. 'Just watch the reins don't get too long, Anna. And Brook, just keep the leg a touch more forward, you'll find it easier to balance.' Livvy had spotted every minute detail of their riding.

They waited for the final pair, Kya and Tilly. They could see from quite a distance that Tilly was riding a very headstrong Magic Spirit. Kya had been adamant that Bastion was going to be stronger, so insisted that she should go in front.

'Very good, Kya,' said Livvy. 'You had Bastion in a lovely rhythm and from what I could see you both looked in great balance. The short stirrups helped,' she reminded Kya.

It was difficult to tell whether Tilly was bright red from exhaustion from trying to hold Magic or whether it was absolute fury towards Kya.

'We could all see you had a horrid time, Tilly,' said Livvy sympathetically, 'but if you are sitting on a very strong horse, keep the hand even lower, or maybe try bridging your reins.'

Tilly could sense Kya smirking.

'The more you pull at a strong horse, the stronger they will get,' Livvy added, directing this advice to all of the juniors.

As they made their way back down the gallops in walk, Brook asked Livvy about her plans for the future.

'I've got quite a few new horses this year, so it's a case of getting to know them. My main hope is obviously Celtic Surprise, who will be aimed at Badminton, if he's ready. Then I have got a couple that I'll take to France to do a three-star event, the next level down from the top four stars. From there I'll go to the top event in Ireland, back on the overnight boat, quick turnaround, and up to a large international event in Yorkshire.'

'Gee, do you ever stop?' asked Harry.

'Boxing Day, if I am lucky,' replied Livvy.

'Not Christmas?' enquired Ben.

'I wish. With less than half our team of staff, it's a very busy day. Plenty to muck out.'

Tilly by now had calmed down and listened intently, imagining what it would be like to take Magic to one of the big European events.

'I'd love to compete abroad at one of those top events,' she said.

'Keep up the hard work and maybe you will,' said Livvy warmly.

Kya sniffed. 'Not on Magic, you won't,' she retorted. 'Doesn't a horse have to have a passport to go abroad?'

Here we go again, thought Tilly. She clutched Magic's reins and urged him forward, out of Kya's range. Kya, however, persisted.

'Isn't that right, Livvy? Horses can only travel if they have the right documents. But unfortunately Tilly doesn't have *any* documents for Magic Spirit . . . because he's not officially hers.'

Tilly stiffened. What was Kya's problem? Why did she have to keep picking on this issue? Anna and Brook spoke up.

'Honestly, Kya, just because Magic hasn't got the bloodlines like Bastion,' said Anna, 'doesn't mean he can't be a contender.'

'And for the record,' said Brook, 'the reason Tilly doesn't have the original documents for Magic is because he was *rescued*.'

Kya scowled, but Tilly sat up straight, gratified that the others had defended her. They reached the bottom of the gallops.

'Okay,' said Livvy, 'we are going up one more time. I want you to open your horses up, push on at the start, then when you get to the steeper hill, ease to half pace.'

'What are we waiting for?' said Ben.

They went in the same order, except, much to Kya's disgust, Livvy said Tilly and Magic should go in front.

Magic sped up to a canter then galloped on, making easy work of the slight incline. Tilly and Magic were equally thrilled by this freedom of speed. Moments later, however, Tilly sensed another horse moving up alongside her – a glossy chestnut coat with light white spotting. Of course, it was Bastion. Kya was trying to overtake. Tilly glanced sideways and caught her eye. Without a second thought, she gave Magic a sharp kick and urged him to go even faster. All of a sudden, the girls were locked in a two-horse race towards the top of the gallops.

Tilly felt she *had* to push Magic, just a little more – otherwise she'd never hear the end of it. She could already imagine the gloating remarks Kya would make about thoroughbreds having more stamina than rescue horses with no documents.

'Go on, Magic! Go on, boy!' she cried.

Magic did all he could, but it wasn't enough. He lost his footing slightly. He veered sideways and nearly knocked into Bastion.

'Whoa!' yelled Kya. 'Control your horse!'

Both the girls were forced to slow down. When they reached the top Livvy gave each of them a stern look.

'I'm all for competition,' she said. 'But I don't approve of recklessness. Be more careful in future.'

Exhausted and shaken, neither of the girls spoke as they walked back to the yard, but it was obvious from their body language that a line had been drawn.

Chapter Five

By the time the group returned to Hancocks, the sun was starting to set. Streaks of orange and purple illuminated the sky. Tilly was already thinking about the list of tasks she had to do before she could relax: untack Magic, brush his saddle, sponge him down, pick out his feet then give him his feed. After such a long and intense day, she was looking forward to crashing in front of the television, but she knew Magic's needs came first. It didn't surprise her, however, to hear Kya complaining to Anna.

'At my school, I just turn up at the stables

and Bastion is ready for me to ride. There's a girl who does all the messy jobs for me. I mean, seriously, this is so annoying.'

Tilly hoped Livvy was listening too, that she would notice Kya's attitude. She was still upset after the jibes about Magic not having a passport and the disastrous gallop. Secretly, she wanted to get back at Kya somehow.

Suddenly, Nick came rushing towards them.

'I'm so glad you're back. I was just about to phone. I'm afraid there's a problem with one of our youngsters,' he said.

Livvy looked up from sponging Evening Star, alarmed.

'Oh, no. Which one?'

'Sorry, Liv. It's your favourite. It's Archie Boy.'

The news caught everyone's attention. They all stopped what they were doing. Tilly glanced at Livvy and saw the concern in her eyes. Her rivalry with Kya immediately seemed petty and insignificant, now that a horse was suffering.

'Where is he? What do you think the matter is?'

'Earlier, one of the grooms noticed he'd developed a runny nose, so we transferred him to the isolation barn. Then he wouldn't have his feed and now he's started coughing and choking.'

Livvy shook her head.

'That's not like Archie Boy. My poor boy! Have you called the vet?'

'She's on her way.'

'Good. Well done. Now, let's go and see him.'

Tilly remembered Archie Boy from the mucking-out session that morning. He'd been a bit naughty, but full of character. She was glad when Livvy suggested that she and the others accompanied her.

'Welcome to the world of event yards,' she said, as they tied up their own horses. 'Nothing can be taken for granted, especially when it comes to health. We take great care in making sure all our horses' immunisations are up to date, but there are no guarantees. That's why it's so important to be hands-on in the stables. The more we keep track of a horse's behaviour, the more likely it is that we'll spot problems as soon as they arise. Hopefully it'll turn out to be nothing serious, but we need to make sure . . . '

They crowded around the entrance to the isolation barn. Nick explained that keeping a sick horse away from others would reduce the risk of illness spreading to the rest of the yard. He opened the stable door and they peered in. Tilly could see Archie Boy, head down, coughing and choking and looking very glum – the opposite of how she'd last seen him. Livvy went up to him and stroked his nose. As soon as she touched him, he gazed at her adoringly.

'Hello, young man,' she said gently. 'What's going on here, then?'

She was tender and kind, so different to the strict Livvy who ran a huge event yard, or the fearless Livvy who charged towards terrifying cross country obstacles. Tilly was starting to see that maybe Livvy's brilliance was because she was able to be all of these things: organised, brave *and* caring.

'Do you think he'll be okay?' said Tilly.

'Well, whatever it is we've caught it early.' She stroked Archie Boy's neck. 'He's one of my rising stars, born and bred here at Hancocks, so he's extra special to me.'

'Does anyone have any ideas what might be wrong?' said Nick, casting his eye across the group.

They looked at each other.

'Check the symptoms,' Nick prompted. 'Refusal to eat. Listless. Runny nose. Coughing a lot.'

'Equine influenza?' suggested Kya.

'Could be,' said Nick. 'Anyone else?'

'Strangles?' said Anna.

'Colic?' said Ben.

'Tetanus?' said Brook.

Tilly gazed at Archie Boy. She'd read hundreds of articles about horse health. Yes, he looked ill, but there was no sign of a temperature, and no other symptoms.

'It might be choke?' she ventured.

The others looked at her as though she wasn't taking the matter seriously.

'Well, that would be a relief,' said Livvy. 'But I guess we'll have to wait for the vet's verdict. Why don't you settle your horses then go back to the farmhouse, and I'll let you know what happens.'

That evening, as the Junior Squad gathered in the kitchen for dinner, all the talk centred around Archie Boy's illness.

'I hope it *isn't* contagious,' said Kya. 'I don't want Bastion getting anything. But as for suggesting it's just choke . . . what a silly thing to say. I mean, that's one of Livvy's favourite horses. He might never recover. He might *die*. Don't you think you should have been more sensitive, Tilly?'

She sneered at Tilly across the table. Tilly did her best to ignore it. Clare, the housekeeper, laid a spread of breads and hams and cheeses in front of them. They tucked in – apart from Kya who nibbled her soya crisps. Minutes later, the door swung open. Livvy and Nick came in. They were both smiling.

'Whoever suggested Archie Boy might have choke should be proud of themselves,' said Livvy. 'The vet confirmed it. It turns out one of our new girls fed him tonight because Karen who normally feeds him had to go to a funeral. The combination of the food not being wet enough and Archie Boy being greedy and eating his food too quickly, caused a partial blockage in the oesophagus, the tube that takes the food from the mouth to the stomach.

'The vet sedated him and then passed a stomach tube via his nostril into the oesophagus which gently encouraged the obstruction to move down into his stomach, so hopefully he'll soon be fit again. The worry is over. Thanks, guys.'

Tilly beamed. Everyone except Kya congratulated her on her clever deduction.

'You really know your stuff, don't you?' said Harry. 'If I ever have a problem with Hunter I'm coming straight to you . . . if that's okay?'

'Yes, it's okay,' Tilly giggled.

'Now, I've got something else to say,' said Livvy, breaking a piece of bread and spreading it with butter. 'Since you've demonstrated that you're all pretty efficient in the saddle – and that there's definitely a competitive air among you,' she glanced at Tilly and Kya as she said this, 'I think we should work towards a combined training competition, which is like an event but without the cross country, so just dressage and show jumping.'

There was a ripple of excited chatter.

'*But*, the catch is that you won't be allowed to compete on your own horse . . . oh no, that would be far too easy. You have to compete on each other's. You can draw lots for who gets to ride who.'

The excitement was immediately replaced by bewilderment.

'Really?' said Ben.

'I don't want to ride anyone else's horse,' said Kya.

'I'll be rubbish if I ride a horse I don't know,' said Anna.

Livvy just shook her head.

'No excuses,' she said.

After tea, they scribbled their names on pieces of paper and threw them into a riding hat. Tilly knew she had good reason to worry. Not about the horse she'd have to ride, but about who got to ride Magic. He wasn't always cooperative with other people. He could play up terribly. Nonetheless, she put her worry aside and delved into the hat. She retrieved a crumpled slip of paper and unfolded it.

'Who've you got?' whispered Brook.

Tilly looked up.

'Bastion!'

'And who've you got, Kya?'

Kya locked eyes on Tilly and pursed her lips.

'Lucky me,' she said sarcastically.

Immediately Tilly knew she'd drawn Magic.

Chapter Six

That evening, despite being tired, Tilly decided to work late around the yard. She didn't want to spend any more time with Kya than she had to, especially now that they were going to be swapping rides for the combined training competition. She pulled on her riding coat and went outside.

Apart from the occasional owl hooting, and the horses shifting comfortably in their stables, it was quiet. The sky was clear and the trees were illuminated by a full moon. Magic was in his stable, rubbing his shoulder on

the wall. As soon as he saw Tilly he pricked his
ears.

'Got an itch?' she asked him.

She went forward and scratched it for him.
When he was satisfied, he turned, rested his
head on her shoulder and peacefully lowered
his eyelids.

'Hello, boy,' said Tilly. 'What a nice welcome!'

As she cradled his velvety nose in her hands,
she dreaded the thought of letting Kya ride
him. She knew she had to go through with it, in
the spirit of fair play. And she certainly didn't
want to let Livvy down. But the idea bothered
her intensely.

'Of *all* people,' she said, 'it would have to be
her, wouldn't it? Well, you'd better behave for
Her Majesty, Magic, or I'll never hear the end of
it. She'll blame me. She'll claim I haven't trained
you properly or something. Or start going on
about you being stolen again.'

She held Magic tighter.

'But you're not stolen, are you, boy?' she
whispered. 'You're mine. We found each other.

We belong together. Oh, Magic, I love you so much.'

She kissed him on the nose, then went into the yard, picked up a broom and started sweeping the concrete. Next she headed to the tack room and began oiling her precious saddle and bridle, checking all the stitching and then polishing her bit rings. She always spent ages on her kit, knowing how expensive it was and how hard her parents had to work to help her with her passion. None of it was particularly dirty, but the task distracted her from thinking about Kya. Once she was done, she began to tidy the rest of the tack room. She untangled straps, straightened saddles, arranged boots and hats into size order, brushed down the benches and gave the whiteboard a thorough clean.

Just as Tilly was finishing, the door of the tack room opened. It was Livvy.

'Oh, hi, Tilly,' she said. 'You're working late. I'm just looking for some clippers. One of my up-and-coming horses is competing at the weekend and it looks as if the weather is going to be warm, so I need to clip her.'

Then she looked around, noticed the tidy equipment, and blinked.

'Wow! This tack room looks immaculate! Did *you* do this?'

Tilly shrugged and smiled.

'Yes, I – I hope you don't mind.'

Livvy laughed.

'Mind? I don't mind at all. When it comes to tidying, I'm afraid some of my girls could do better. I have to nag them all the time. It drives me mad. But you, *you* Tilly, something tells me *you're* different. Thank you. If you're not too exhausted, maybe you'd like to help me do some clipping?'

Tilly grinned.

Livvy collected her clippers and showed Tilly to one of the stables.

'Meet Gladys, short for Glad Times. If Archie recovers from his choke, which the vet says he will, I plan to take him and Gladys to Elmhurst Horse Trials.'

Elmhurst Horse Trials was the most local of

events, and though it was low key it was a great place to take the babies.

'Could you just grab a head collar for me, please?' Livvy asked, as she opened the stable door. Tilly peered inside. A tall, elegant black mare gazed back at her. She slipped the head collar on, and picked the mare's feet out before leading her out of the stable.

'Follow me,' said Livvy, directing Tilly towards the clipping and washing down box. It was an empty stable with a special rubber floor to stop the horses from slipping. More importantly, it acted as a safety insulator. Without it, if a horse was to tread on and cut through the lead of the clippers, their steel shoes would act as a conductor and they could be electrocuted.

'She knows what's coming,' said Livvy. 'She's a good girl. She always tries her best to please, she is a very honest mare.'

She handed Tilly the clippers, switched on the fluorescent light strip, then tied Gladys up on the pillar reins – so she had a rope clipped on both sides of her head collar tied to rings on two opposite walls.

'Have you ever clipped a horse on your own before?'

'Only Magic. And I've helped Angela clip other horses. She's the owner of Silver Shoe Farm, where Magic is stabled.'

'I know Angela,' replied Livvy, smiling. 'We've been friends since we were juniors together.'

'Really?'

'Oh, yes. It's a small world. If you become a three-day event rider, you're never too far from a friend . . . '

Tilly sensed she meant something by this. Was she talking about Kya? Did she know they'd fallen out? She didn't say anything. She didn't want Livvy to think she couldn't get along with her team mates.

Livvy turned on the clippers. Gladys instantly raised her head, snorting.

'I will just let her settle and get used to the noise before I start clipping. Good lady,' Livvy said, in a calm, reassuring voice, holding the clippers in one hand and stroking Gladys' neck with the other. Responding to Livvy's reassurance, Gladys quickly relaxed and lowered her head. 'Now we're ready to start.'

Livvy started to clip Gladys' large, sloping shoulder.

'It's best to start clipping an area that isn't too tickly, so it gives them a chance to get used to it first,' she explained, while keeping a constant pressure on the clippers so she didn't leave marks as she clipped. 'I don't want her looking like a zebra with stripes everywhere.'

This reminded Tilly of Stripy, the zebra foal, who she'd helped rescue when she was on her riding safari.

Livvy neatly clipped some very straight leg lines, leaving the hair on Gladys's legs but just trimming the feathers off her heels.

Livvy worked away clipping Gladys' athletic body while Tilly stood close to her head giving her the odd polo reward. They talked in extra loud voices so they could hear themselves over the constant buzz of the clippers. Livvy told Tilly about her plans for the new horses and Tilly chatted away about Silver Shoe and her own riding hopes.

'When I was little,' she said, 'I used to daydream about riding your horse, Evening Star.'

'That's funny,' said Livvy. 'You're not the only one. Over the years, I've had thousands of letters from young girls and boys saying the same thing.'

'And have you ever let any of them?' said Tilly, hopefully.

'Goodness, no. He's not the sort of horse you'd unleash on an inexperienced junior. I'm glad he's been such an inspiration to people, but the truth is, he can be a handful. He's no Pony Club fun ride, that's for sure.'

'Oh.'

'And I guess I might be a little territorial. I mean, I've had so much success with him. The thought of letting someone else ride him . . . anyway, tell me about Magic. I heard

Brook say he's a rescue horse?'

'Um, yes, kind of,' said Tilly. 'It was me who rescued him. We've been partners ever since.'

She glanced at the ceiling.

'And one day I'd like us to reach the top . . . three-star and four-star events. Just like you.'

'Well, you're on the right track,' said Livvy.

'Yes, except . . . I don't know . . . with Magic being a rescue horse and everything.'

'It doesn't have to be about where you start,' said Livvy. 'It's about where you end up.'

Tilly thought about this then smiled.

'Yes,' she said. 'Yes, I suppose it is.'

'Just the tricky areas now.' Livvy talked quietly to Gladys in her gentle voice. She started to clip very carefully under her tummy and between her legs. Gladys never moved. Livvy unclipped the ropes and left her untied for the final part.

'I don't want her pulling back and frightening herself when I do her head, but if you stand by her ready to hold on if she starts to move.'

Tilly immediately moved towards Gladys' head. She was so good to do, apart from a few little twitches and sneezes when the hair fell down her face and tickled her nose.

'We have done well, Tilly, to get her done without any outside help.'

'What do you mean?' asked Tilly.

'If any horses are that worried or difficult to clip, I call the vet in to come and give them a sedative, it's much easier, kinder and safer,' Livvy said.

'One has to be so careful when clipping, I have heard of so many accidents with people getting kicked, not just from their hind legs, but also horses striking out with their front legs. So never stand directly in front of them.'

Tilly went back to the farmhouse with renewed confidence after her chat with Livvy. She found the others in the living room, watching a movie.

'Hi, Tilly,' called Brook.

'Hiya.'

'Well, Tilly,' said Kya, 'you know you've missed most of the movie? It's nearly finished. Where've you been?'

'Just . . . around.'

Kya turned to Anna.

'I bet she's been creeping to Livvy again,' she whispered, loud enough for Tilly to hear. 'Either that or she's been squeezing in extra riding. I mean, let's face it, intense practice is the only way a rescue horse is going to have a chance against a team of thoroughbreds.'

Anna pulled a face and told Kya to stop being nasty. Tilly, meanwhile, told herself not to rise to it. No way. She wasn't going to let Kya or anything Kya said bring her down. Not after the lovely things Livvy had said. Instead, she trudged up the stairs, brushed her teeth, pulled her pyjamas on and crawled into bed.

Under the covers, she took out her phone. It had been a long day, but an interesting one. Yawning, she tapped on the email icon and opened her inbox. She was about to start typing a message to her parents, to tell them what she'd been up to, when . . . there it was. An email, *the* email – the one she'd dreaded, the one that could change everything.

Chapter Seven

To Miss Tiger Lily Redbrow,

My name is Fred Webb. I own Dawson's Farm on the
North Cosford border. You do not know me, but I
believe you know my horse. I have received information
suggesting that you are riding a 16.1 hh grey gelding with
a distinctive dapple that you are calling Magic Spirit.
I would be interested to know the exact details of his
origins, as I lost a horse that fits his exact description a
few years ago. He would have been four years old at the
time. Please contact me urgently regarding this matter.

Yours sincerely,

Fred Webb

P.S. If you are in any doubt, I have his registration and other documents to prove my ownership.

Tilly read the email, then read it again. A cold, heavy dread washed over her. She gripped her horsehair bracelets, especially the one made from Magic's tail.

'No,' she whispered. 'Please. No.'

Her hands started to tremble. She cupped them over her mouth and checked the date of the message. It had been sent that afternoon. There were no contact details other than an email address. Fred Webb? Who was Fred Webb? She didn't recognise the name or know of the farm, but his description of Magic was worryingly accurate.

That said, anyone could get an idea of Magic's appearance just by looking at photos on the Pony Club website, but it was the reference to Magic's age that made Tilly nervous. Angela had guessed Magic was about four years old when they'd taken him in. How could Fred Webb know that, unless his claim was *true*?

And although the email didn't specifically say he wanted Magic back, it was obvious from the fact that he was claiming he had documents to prove ownership. Tilly's eyes filled with tears.

Eventually, she switched off her phone, lay back, and stared at the ceiling. It was too much to take in. She remembered how Kya had gone on and *on* about Magic not having any official papers, as though it was such a big deal. Tilly had tried to downplay it. In *her* mind, what had mattered most was that she loved Magic and Magic loved her. Suddenly, she heard a noise on the stairs and realised the others were coming up to bed. She didn't want to talk, so she rolled over and pretended to be asleep, but as she closed her eyes, a horrible thought occurred to her. What if Kya had something to do with the email? What if Kya was the one who'd tipped off Fred Webb?

After an uneasy night, Tilly was up before the alarm clock rang. She got dressed quietly, without waking Anna or Kya, crept out to the yard, and went straight to Magic's stable. He was waiting for her at the door so she gave him the biggest hug she could and fed him a carrot.

'Oh, Magic,' she said, scratching his favourite itchy spot at the base of his neck.

He nuzzled her neck and sniffed her pockets, his little habit, hunting for treats. She found a mint, which he crunched eagerly. She knew him so well – and he knew her. Moments later, there was a clatter outside. Brook came into the stable corridor with a wheelbarrow and a fork.

'Hey, you,' he said softly. 'You're up early.'

'You too,' said Tilly.

'I want to get a head start. I can't wait for the combined training competition, can you?'

Tilly murmured. Brook pulled a face and stepped towards her.

'Is everything okay? I don't want to pry, but it's not like you not to be excited about a competition, especially when Livvy James is the judge.'

Tilly sighed, then started to sob.

'Oh, Brook, something awful has happened. I don't know what to do.'

She told him all about the email. Brook listened and shook his head.

'But you never know,' he said, 'it might be a hoax. It might be someone who's read an article about you and Magic in the local paper and wants to cash in. I'm sure you realise that now Magic has started showing potential, he's worth a lot more money. And money makes people greedy. Maybe it's just a con trick?'

'Maybe,' said Tilly, looking doubtful.

'Whatever it is, don't worry, sis,' said Brook, wrapping her in a hug. 'We'll get to the bottom of this. No one's taking Magic away from you – not without a fight, anyhow.'

'Thanks,' she sniffed. 'I knew I could count on you.'

'Come on. Let's get on with the rest of this training week and make sure we make the most of it, then we'll deal with this email as soon as we get home. Isn't Kya riding Magic today? You'll have to get him groomed to perfection, to match her royal standards.'

Tilly rolled her eyes.

'Don't joke,' she said. 'You know she's got it in for me. I'm fed up of her. And part of me wonders if she had anything to do with the email . . .'

'Kya? She may be a stuck-up drama-queen, but she wouldn't do anything *that* mean. Surely?'

Taking Brook's advice, Tilly did what she could to focus on the day ahead, one task at a time. After feeding Magic and mucking out his stable, she took his rug off and gave him a good brush, combed his mane and brushed through his tail making sure she removed all the shavings. Tired from her fretful night, she yawned her way through the work but, nonetheless, she was determined not to give Kya anything to complain about. Magic would be the best groomed horse on the yard.

Once his coat was gleaming, she picked out his feet. As the dressage and jumping was all going to be on grass rather than in the sand area, she decided – for extra stability – to add studs to his shoes. She didn't want Kya moaning that he was slipping the whole time. Magic stood patiently and lifted each foot in turn. When it came to the last one, however, his off hind (right back leg), Tilly took hold of his leg and the stress caught up with her again.

As she held his hoof in her hands and picked the dirt out of the stud hole with a nail, she remembered that day – the day she'd rescued him. She had a vision of his weak, under-nourished frame, his flea-infested coat and the cuts on his legs. He'd seemed like a horse with no hope. Yet, she'd given him hope. He'd looked into her eyes, seen a kind person and given her his trust. How could anyone want to take him away from her?

Eyes full of tears, she tugged at Magic's shoe and started screwing the studs in. She wiped her cheeks, and tightened the studs. But her mind wasn't on the job. She had forgotten to use the 'T tap', a special tool which clears the dirt out of the thread, so that the studs screw in correctly. She didn't notice that a couple of them weren't properly threaded. She was too full of worry.

Chapter Eight

The first phase in the combined training competition was dressage. Straight after breakfast, the squad gathered outside the tack room. Livvy gave them a sheet of paper with the dressage test written on it. They read it through. As they hadn't ridden each other's horses before, Livvy had given them a very basic test that was to be executed in an international-sized 20m × 60m grass arena, bigger than the smaller 20m × 40m arena that they were used to. The dressage test would involve entering and halting from trot at X, medium trots and

82

serpentines on both reins, canter with medium canter circles, again on both reins, with a free rein walk halfway through the test, all moves that Tilly and Magic had practised endlessly. But this time, of course, Tilly wasn't riding Magic. She was riding Bastion. There was no time to practise and with all the worry about Fred Webb's email, her concentration levels were flagging.

Having all had twenty minutes to get to know their new mounts, Anna took the test first, riding Ben's horse, Hedgehunter. She did well to handle him, considering his size. Ben, in turn, rode Matinee, who was increasingly frisky and didn't complete the last movement. Harry rode Brook's horse, Solo. He managed to complete everything in the right order. Livvy congratulated him, but took marks off for lopsided circles. Next, Brook took his turn on Harry's chestnut stallion, Nobleman. Brook had a nightmare. Nobleman seemed bewildered by having someone other than Harry on his back. His medium trots were erratic and his stride was uneven. Tilly knew Brook liked his dressage to be perfect, but luckily he saw the funny side.

'Nobleman has clearly decided I'm not noble enough for him!' he said, dismounting. 'But maybe we'll get on better when we jump.'

He looked at Harry.

'Well done,' he said. 'You handled Solo brilliantly. You've obviously got the knack.'

'Thanks,' said Harry.

Tilly smiled. That's how it should be, she thought. Good sportsmanship. Team work. Even though Brook hadn't done well, he still had the grace to congratulate Harry. She glanced at Kya, and caught her eye. Kya gave her a smile, but it wasn't a friendly one. It was an 'I'll show *you*' kind of smile. Tilly hugged her arms to her middle and felt sick with worry.

'Okay,' said Livvy. 'Tilly, you're up next, riding Bastion. Ready?'

Tilly took a breath and nodded. She rode Bastion around the outside of the white-boarded grass arena, awaiting her signal to start. She'd always admired Dutch horses. She couldn't deny that Bastion was a beautiful type – his elegant face and athletic limbs, his poise and genuine temperament – but ultimately, he didn't feel like Magic. When she looked back and saw Magic waiting at the edge, watching her, she was swamped with sadness. If it hurt her to be apart from him for a brief competition, how would it feel if he was taken from her permanently?

'Tilly,' Livvy prompted. 'It's time to start. You wouldn't keep the judges waiting in a real competition situation, would you?'

'Um, no. Of course not.'

Tilly nudged Bastion forward. They entered at a working trot and proceeded down the centre line. Thankfully, Bastion didn't share his owner's dislike of Tilly. His stride was supple and rhythmic and he obliged with only the lightest of aids. He tracked left then began the first circle. Tilly felt good again, doing what she loved, effortlessly. But as she prepared to change rein and let Bastion free walk, she noticed Kya sniggering and her confidence collapsed. Her mind went blank and she couldn't remember the rest of the moves. Bastion twitched, waiting for her command, trotted a few paces then came to a halt. She could feel everyone watching her, wondering what was going on.

'I'm sorry,' she said. 'I – I've forgotten. I've forgotten the rest.'

Livvy looked disappointed.

'Oh, well,' she said. 'It was good while it lasted, Tilly. I would like to have seen you complete the full test, but, another time, perhaps?'

Embarrassed, Tilly walked Bastion to the exit. She kept her head down. She didn't want to speak to anyone, not even Brook or Harry. She just wanted to be with Magic. But Magic, her beautiful Magic, was now being ridden around the outside of the arena by Kya.

Tilly watched from the corner of her eye.

'How can I possibly ride through a test in a jumping saddle?' Kya huffed.

Tilly felt embarrassed by the fact the Magic was the only horse not to have his own dressage saddle. She knew all the sacrifices that her parents had made to enable her to pursue her dream. She couldn't keep asking for more, so she managed to do everything with the one saddle.

She quickly realised, however, that Magic was being as true as ever, loyal to his Tilly. It was a struggle for Kya to even get him into the arena. He was spooking at all the dressage letters. When she finally got him in, he showed no interest in following her aids. He stood motionless over X, refusing to move, ignoring all her attempts to urge him forward. Eventually, out of frustration, Kya resorted to using her voice, which got him moving, but at a cost – marks would inevitably be deducted for using vocal aid. She struggled through the rest of the test looking red-faced and flustered. And while Tilly felt bad to admit it, she was glad.

Next came the show jumping. They nipped back to the yard to change tack.

'You are okay, you don't need to swap saddles,' Kya sarcastically reminded Tilly.

'But I do need to put a running martingale on him,' replied Tilly, red with humiliation and feeling even more dispirited by Kya's constant digging.

They led their horses back to the show jumping paddock which wasn't quite as flat as the neighbouring dressage paddock and with the added difficulty that it was wet and slippery from the heavy overnight rain.

Nick had been up early that morning setting out a course for them to jump. Livvy had a full set of jumps, consisting of brightly coloured poles and fillers, water trays, she even had a pair of tall jump stands that were made to look like red letterboxes, similar to the ones at the last Olympics.

They took it in turns to hold the horses and walk the course. Livvy walked it with them, giving them useful tips and advice about how to ride it correctly and with feel, bearing in mind they were on unfamiliar horses.

'It may not seem very big to you guys,' said Livvy, 'but it's important that because we are swapping horses we don't want to jeopardise anyone's, horse's or rider's, confidence.'

'A true horseman is not someone who is able to ride one particular horse,' she went on, 'it's someone who is able to climb on many and be able to feel, and work out, how a horse thinks, someone who's able to adapt to the different characters.'

The juniors realised the importance of what she was saying. They were well aware that the very top riders who lasted a long time in the sport were the riders who, over the years, were able to ride horses of all different shapes and sizes.

They warmed up together popping a vertical and, when Livvy was happy with that, she added a back rail and turned it into a small parallel.

'Remember, less is more, by that I mean the stiller and quieter you can sit, the less you interfere with the horse's balance.'

They competed in the same order as they'd done dressage. Anna was first, on Hedgehunter. She rocketed around the course, only to discover she'd taken a wrong turn and missed out the double.

'You see, it's not just about clearing the fences,' said Livvy. 'You've got to have your wits about you, concentrate at all times. Imagine how many wrong turns you could take, galloping around a cross country course?'

Anna nodded and sighed.

'Bad luck,' said Brook.

'At least you won't make that mistake again,' said Ben.

Ben jumped Matinee, followed by Harry on Solo. They both jumped clear, without taking any wrong turns, but Ben was too gung-ho and Harry was a bit slow and steady.

'Now we need a bit more pace,' said Livvy. 'Time penalties need to be avoided if you're serious about winning. I'm looking for the rider who knows how to be careful, but quick as well.'

Brook was next to take on the course, with Nobleman. From the moment they set off, Tilly could tell they were going to go well. Brook had a determined look on his face and Nobleman had a good active canter. Sure enough, they produced a good time leaving every jump up. Everyone cheered as he leaned forward rewarding Nobleman with a big pat.

'Yes, that's how it should be done!' said Livvy. 'Impressive riding, Brook! Congratulations!'

'What's your secret?' said Harry. 'I'd love it if Nobleman went like that every time.'

'I guess I try not to interfere too much,' said Brook. 'I just kept riding him forward and allowed him to get on with it. It's what I do with Solo.'

As the boys exchanged riding tips, Tilly

mounted Bastion. Hoping she could replicate Brook's success, she took a deep breath and cleared her mind. While she was out there, she just wanted to focus on the course.

'Go for it!' said Livvy encouragingly.

It felt as though Livvy wanted her to do well, that she'd been genuinely disappointed that Tilly had messed up the dressage.

'Come on then, Bastion,' said Tilly, leaning forward. 'Let's show them we can do this!'

She nudged with her leg and Bastion obeyed and went into canter. The first jump, a yellow and green parallel, came up. The run-up was muddy, which slowed them down, but Bastion still managed an extravagant jump and was on to the next before Tilly had a chance to praise him. He was keen but his technique was different to Magic's. He jumped really high, even over low obstacles. She balanced him quickly on the turns which prevented him from slipping too much.

As she cleared the last fence everyone applauded. Tilly was pleased. It wasn't the best round of her life – she was saving that for Magic – but in the middle of all her stress, she'd proved to herself that she could handle an unfamiliar horse around a show jumping course. She'd done herself proud.

'Well done, Tilly,' said Livvy. 'Okay, Kya and Magic, now you.'

Kya and Magic cantered around the arena a couple of times before they started, as they'd had the longest wait. He seemed more cooperative than he had been during the dressage. Tilly hoped this was because he adored jumping and not because he was getting used to Kya.

'That ground is getting more cut up and slippery,' said Anna, as Kya headed towards the first fence.

'It is,' said Tilly. 'I wouldn't worry, though. The horses seem to be coping with it.'

But as soon as she'd said it, an uneasy feeling came over her. For some reason, she felt the need to sit up and watch closely. She tracked Magic's footfall, the turn of his hooves as he worked up to speed. Then it happened. Halfway through a turn, one of Magic's hind legs buckled beneath him. He skidded and tumbled and landed hard on his side. Kya flew out of the saddle and, with one foot still hooked in the stirrup, hit the ground.

There was a moment of horrified silence, then a flurry of noise and activity.

'Oh, no! Magic!' Tilly cried, her hand over her mouth.

She jumped down from Bastion, threw the reins at Brook, felt the cold rush of adrenalin through her arms and legs. She immediately followed Livvy, who started running towards the accident. She could hear Brook and Anna calling for her to wait, but she couldn't stop. She couldn't hold back. She had to get to Magic. He was lying down, looking scared and startled.

Get up, she willed him. *Please, Magic, get up! And please let Kya be okay!*

All she could think was 'What if Magic is injured?', but as soon as Magic saw Tilly he rolled and staggered to his feet. No sign of a limp or a scratch. He shook his head, gave a great whinny, then advanced towards her, thrust his head into her arms and let her hold him.

'Oh, Magic!' she sobbed. 'I'm so glad you got up. I'm so glad you're okay.'

Then she heard a scream. Kya!

Tilly could see Kya was alert – *very* alert – but she was still on the ground. Livvy was kneeling at her side, trying to keep her calm, while she spoke on her phone. Anna gave Hunter to Ben and rushed over to Kya.

'OW!' Kya cried. 'It hurts! It *hurts*!'

'What hurts?' said Anna. 'Which bit of you hurts?'

'All of me!'

Tilly gripped Magic's reins tightly and felt guilt rise inside her. She felt terrible about the fact that Kya had fallen off Magic, her horse – especially since she'd been secretly glad that he'd been difficult for her during the dressage. She'd *wanted* things to go wrong for them. Not *this* wrong.

Livvy ordered Kya to lie still, then came over to check on Magic.

'Does he seem okay?' she asked. 'When we get him back to the yard, we'll have everything checked properly.'

'He seems all right,' said Tilly, trying to sound positive. 'But is Kya okay?'

'It's hard to tell. It wasn't one of the worst falls I've seen, but she's very distressed. We've called an ambulance to be on the safe side.'

Tilly sniffed and gulped.

'The thing that puzzles me,' said Livvy, 'is how on earth it happened? It's as though Magic went down for no obvious reason . . .'

She walked around, inspecting Magic, looking for answers. She checked his front legs, then his hind quarters.

'Well, here's the problem!' she snapped.

She held up one of Magic's hind legs.

'Poorly threaded studs!'

Tilly blinked.

'One stud has come out completely and the other has worked its way loose! So, who's responsible for this? Who put these studs in?'

'I – I did,' said Tilly. 'Um, I did them earlier. I wanted to make sure . . .'

She was so shocked and ashamed she couldn't finish her sentence. Livvy remained stern.

'Oh, Tilly. You didn't do it properly. You weren't concentrating, were you? Do you realise how dangerous this is?'

'Yes,' said Tilly, tearfully, remembering how tired and distracted she'd been when she'd groomed Magic that morning. 'Yes. Please. I'm so sorry. I didn't mean . . .'

'You'd better take Magic back to the stables while we wait for the ambulance,' said Livvy crossly. 'Go with her, please, Brook. Then find Nick and tell him what's happened. We'll talk about it later.'

They led their horses from the scene. As they walked, however, Tilly looked back over her shoulder. Kya was still on the ground, howling, but when she saw Tilly she managed to turn her head. She looked Tilly directly in the eye, collected herself and yelled.

'This is *your* fault. And, you know what? I bet you did it *deliberately*!'

Chapter Nine

Nick took his time, running his hands across every inch of Magic's legs, back and neck. Tilly and Brook stood watching in silence, their breath quick and tense.

'That's it,' said Nick, eventually. 'He's in the clear. Not a mark on him. Lucky boy!'

He gave Magic a pat. Tilly sighed with relief.

'Thank you,' she said.

'You might want to give his legs a hose down though, just to soothe any tenderness and help prevent any inflammation. We must keep a close eye on him and check there is no swelling in the morning.'

'Sure,' said Tilly, handing Magic a mint from her pocket. 'Thank goodness, boy. I'm so pleased you're not hurt.'

Nick brushed his hands down his shirt.

'Well, I'd better get on. Several horses need moving and a feed delivery has just arrived. I don't know how long Livvy's going to be at the hospital, so it's all hands on deck.'

'We can help,' said Tilly.

Nick shook his head.

'I think you've had enough drama for one day. Why don't you go and get something to eat and drink with the others at the farmhouse. You both look shattered.'

The atmosphere in the farmhouse kitchen was solemn. Ben, Anna and Harry were sitting round the table, but no one was joking or laughing as they had on previous evenings. The housekeeper had laid out tea and cake, but none of it had been touched. Tilly walked in behind Brook and felt three sets of eyes track her steps. It was obvious they'd all been talking about her. She sat, pulled her chair in, and chewed her plait nervously.

Brook broke the silence.

'Hi,' he said.

'All right,' said Harry. 'So, what's happening?'

'Magic's fine,' said Brook. 'Nick checked him over. No injuries. Any news on Kya?'

Harry shuffled awkwardly in his chair.

'Nothing yet,' he said. 'We're waiting.'

Normally, when Harry saw Tilly, he gave her a smile. This time he didn't even catch her eye.

Anna sighed and glanced at her watch.

'Why haven't we had any news yet?' she said anxiously. 'We should have heard *something* by now . . .'

'Maybe the doctors are still assessing her,' said Brook.

'For *this* long?' said Ben. 'The ambulance

left three hours ago. If it's nothing serious they would have discharged her already.'

'Whether it's serious or not, hospitals never take chances with riding accidents,' said Brook. 'I had a fall when I first started competing with Solo. Even though I thought I was fine, the hospital did loads of tests to make sure I didn't have any hidden neck or spinal injuries.'

'And did you?' said Harry, wide-eyed.

'I broke my collar bone,' said Brook, shrugging. 'But that was it.'

'If he'd been unlucky enough to get a neck or spine injury,' said Ben, 'he wouldn't be riding *now*, would he?'

Anna frowned.

'Poor Kya,' she said. 'She winds me up sometimes' – her gaze shifted to Tilly – 'but I *still* like her. I don't want her to be hurt. And she's a great rider. We need her on the team. I just hope she's okay. I mean, if it *does* turn out to be bad news . . .'

'It won't,' said Brook.

He gave Tilly a reassuring nudge, but although no one had said it aloud yet, it was obvious that the thought was there, hanging in the air, like an unpleasant odour. *Had* Tilly loosened Magic's studs deliberately? Had she intended for Kya to mess up? Had *she* caused the accident?

Even though Tilly knew the truth – that she'd never deliberately put Magic or Kya or anyone else in harm's way – she realised how suspicious it looked. Everyone knew she and Kya didn't get on. They'd seen the spark of rivalry during yesterday's hack. They had every reason to question the situation. And if *they* did, what if Livvy did too? What if Livvy James, Tilly's number one eventing heroine, a rider she'd admired all her life, now considered Tilly to be a reckless liability?

Tilly picked up a mug of steaming tea, but her hands were trembling so much, she put it down again. She felt as if she was going to explode with frustration. She hated the way everyone was frowning and sighing and avoiding the obvious. Ben coughed. Anna checked her watch again.

'Just *say* it!' she eventually snapped. 'Why don't you all just say *it*?'

She stood up, balled her hands into fists.

'You think I did this, don't you? You think I did it deliberately? Well, I didn't, all right? I'd never!'

But before anyone could respond, she ran from the room, out into the yard, with her heart racing and her eyes streaming.

The stable block was peaceful. Most of the horses were resting or munching hay. Tilly unbolted the door to Magic's stable. She was so upset, but as soon as she saw Magic's calm face, she felt better. He came towards her. He knew something was wrong – he always did. He leaned his nose over her shoulder and gave a gentle snort.

'It's not fair, Magic! No one believes me.

They think I messed up your studs deliberately. But I'd never put you in danger. *Never*. I'm so sorry, boy. I wasn't concentrating when I put the studs in, I admit that. I wasn't thinking straight, but it was only because I was worried . . .'

She burst into sobs again. Magic closed his eyes and nuzzled her cheek, almost trying to wipe her tears for her.

'It's all going wrong!' she cried. 'Kya's still in hospital. Livvy James is cross and probably thinks I'm a horrible cheat. And so does everyone else. But the thing that's scaring me the most, Magic, the thing that terrifies me, is that someone wants to take you from me. Someone wants you back.'

Tilly buried her face in Magic's shoulder. He didn't move or twitch. He just let her hug him for as long as she needed to, in the quiet of the stables. They only moved apart when Brook appeared.

'Hey, sis,' he whispered. 'I thought I'd find you here.'

He put one hand on Tilly's shoulder and ran the other along Magic's mane.

'He's looking after you, isn't he?' he added.

Tilly nodded.

'He's a sensitive horse with a big heart. Just like Solo. They're more than just tools for competing on, aren't they? They're our best friends. We love them like family.'

'Definitely.'

'Listen, I know you didn't deliberately loosen the studs, Tilly. I believe you. And the others do too. They're just a bit shocked still.'

'But what about Kya? What if her injuries are serious? What if they affect her riding career?'

Tilly could feel herself getting worked up again. Brook took her hands and squeezed.

'Wait and see,' he said.

'But it's *my* fault. Even though it wasn't intentional, it was still me who messed up the studs. If she never rides again, I won't be able to forgive myself.'

'Tilly!' said Brook. 'Stop upsetting yourself.'

Then he dropped his voice to a whisper.

'Trust me,' he said. 'I have a sneaking suspicion that Kya's going to be fine.'

'What? How? What do you know?'

Brook shrugged.

'As I was standing beside you and Magic, I was watching her, and . . . I don't know . . . there was just something really fake about the way she was screaming and howling. It seemed a bit too dramatic, you know? And at one point I swear she was enjoying all the fuss and attention.'

Tilly sniffed, wiping her cheeks on her sleeve.

'Really?'

'I didn't say anything in front of the others. Let's just keep it between us, eh? But you wait, Tilly, she'll be fine. Everything's going to be okay.'

He gave her a hug.

'Are you coming back to the farmhouse with me?' he said.

'Um, not yet,' said Tilly. 'I think I'll hose Magic's legs, then I might just stay with him for a bit.'

'Okay, but if you need me, you know where I am.'

'Thanks.'

Chapter Ten

That night, Tilly didn't go back to the farmhouse at all. She hosed Magic's legs, took him back to his stable, fed him some oats, then snuggled beside him as he lay down on his thick bed of shavings. She hadn't planned to stay there for long, but he was so warm and she was so tired from all the stress, she closed her eyes and started to drift.

She was woken at dawn, by the sound of shuffling hooves and the crowing of a cockerel.

'Uh! Where am I?'

She yawned and stretched, rubbed her eyes, pulled wood shavings from her hair.

'Oh, hello, Magic! I must have . . .'

She looked at her watch.

'5.30! I've been here all night!'

Suddenly, the barn door creaked. Tilly looked up and saw a tall person-shaped silhouette in the morning light, a saddle hooked over one arm and a riding hat on the other. It spoke.

'Fancy a ride?'

'Me?' said Tilly.

The figure stepped forward. It was Livvy.

'Yes, you. Since you slept in the stable all night, I thought you'd be raring to go.'

She came in and stroked Magic's nose.

'I must say I've only ever stayed in a stable all night when I had a very sick horse. My parents thought I was mad, but I liked being close to my horses. It is our duty if they are sick or if I was worried about them. Doesn't make for a very good night's sleep though, does it?'

'No,' said Tilly, feeling the stiffness in her shoulders and neck.

'It's a bit early and I know the yard work shift is about to begin, but I wondered if you and Magic would like to come for a ride with me and Evening Star?'

'And the others too?'

'No. Just us.'

Tilly gasped. She had been worried about Livvy's opinion of her, since the disaster yesterday. But a private ride? This was an honour.

'Get him tacked up, then I'll meet you in the yard in ten, he can have his hay and feed after we've ridden.'

'Okay,' said Tilly.

She jumped to her feet and brushed herself down. She fetched Magic's tack. She brushed him and popped his bridle on, followed by his saddle, and led him into the morning light.

Livvy was waiting at the gate. Evening Star was looking as impressive as ever.

'I love to hack out first thing, before anyone else is up. It's so tranquil at this time of day. The world belongs entirely to us. Let's head for the hill.'

'Sounds good,' said Tilly, still a little unsure what Livvy had in mind.

She adjusted the strap of her riding hat, rested her foot in the stirrup and swung lightly onto Magic's back.

'Ready?'

They walked down the lane, then across the field. Livvy was right. The whole countryside was waking up and it felt as if it was happening just for them. Rabbits hopped across their path. A flock of crows scattered from the trees.

'I wanted to talk to you,' said Livvy. 'I think the most important thing I need to say is that Kya is fine. I brought her back to the farm late last night, with nothing more than a bruise on her hip and a graze on her elbow. It took ages in the hospital. They had to do tests to make sure she had no hidden spine, neck or internal injuries. It was difficult for the doctors to know what was going on, because although she looked okay, she was complaining about all kinds of different pain.'

'Oh? Oh, well, I'm really glad it turned out to be nothing bad.'

'Between you and me, Tilly,' said Livvy, 'I think a lot of it was just for attention.'

Tilly smiled and thought about what Brook had said.

'We would have told you last night,' said Livvy, 'but when we found you asleep next to Magic, we decided to leave you to it. Brook said you'd been very upset. But rest assured, Kya is fine – nothing worse than a dent to her pride. This doesn't, of course, mean you're off the hook.'

Tilly shivered, waited for the reprimand.

'Efficiency and thoroughness are vital to me,' said Livvy. 'There's no room for error in a busy stable yard. When it comes to the horses, we check every detail. We make sure everything is done correctly.'

'I know,' said Tilly, ashamed.

'Failing to secure Magic's stud was a

major error. Although everyone is fine, the consequences could have been serious. Kya, or Magic for that matter, could have been badly injured.'

'I know.'

'But the question *I* want answering is: are you the kind of person who makes a mistake and learns from it, Tilly? Or does your pride tell you to forget it ever happened?'

Tilly knew the answer without having to think about it. She rode up alongside Livvy and looked her directly in the eye.

'I want a career working with horses more than anything,' she said, her heart thumping fast. 'I want to go as far as I can in eventing. I want to *make* it. I know I've made a few mistakes so far . . . and to be honest, I guess I'll probably make more . . . but I promise you, Livvy, I'll *never* make the same mistake twice. I'll learn.'

As she said this, she realised a film of tears had filled her eyes. She blinked, embarrassed, then noticed Livvy looking a bit teary too.

'Oh, Tilly! That's what I hoped you'd say.

You remind me so much of myself when I was your age. So much passion and determination. You say you'll learn and I believe you.'

'I will,' said Tilly. 'I really will.'

Suddenly, she could feel the weight of her worry lifting. To hear Livvy say nice things, to know that she had faith in her – it meant so much. They walked to the bottom of the hill and stopped. The sun had risen high and the air was sweet with the smell of wild flowers. Tilly patted Magic and smiled.

'Listen,' said Livvy. 'I was wondering, I know you have your commitment to Silver Shoe Farm, but I've seen a spark in you that I'm really impressed with. If it's all right with Angela, maybe you'd like to spend a couple of extra weekends at Hancocks, helping out, taking on a few grooming duties?'

Tilly gasped.

'I'd love it!'

'And another thing . . . I know you've always wanted to ride Evening Star . . . so maybe we should swap, just for a little while?'

'Now?'

'No time like the present.'

Tilly gasped again, then dismounted before Livvy could change her mind. She thought of the times she'd lain on her bed, gazing at Evening Star's poster, imagining what it would be like to ride him. They swapped reins. As Tilly looked up, she was a little daunted by the chestnut's huge frame, but Livvy urged her to climb on.

'He'll only need a light touch, so take it easy,' said Livvy. 'Walk on. I'll follow.'

Tilly nudged him forward with her leg. Evening Star lifted his head, snorted and walked forward. Livvy, meanwhile, mounted Magic and rode up beside them. For once, Magic seemed quite agreeable to the idea of having someone other than Tilly in the saddle.

'He must like you,' said Tilly. 'He can be a bit of a pickle with people he doesn't know. I think it's something to do with him being a rescue horse.'

Livvy leaned forward and patted Magic's shoulder.

'Ah, he's doing all right,' she said.

Tilly paused and tensed. Fred Webb's email suddenly shadowed her thoughts.

'You see, I don't think he was very well treated before Angela took him in,' she explained.

'Well, he's a very well treated horse now,' said Livvy. 'And there's no reason why he can't be a champion one day, regardless of what anyone says to you about him.'

'Thanks,' said Tilly. 'I hope you're right.'

They turned up the hill, into the sun. It was a perfect morning for a ride. So despite everything, despite the worry, Tilly decided she would hold on to the hope that Magic's future was indeed with her and no one else. She made herself a silent promise that she would find a way to keep him always, no matter what.

Pippa Funnell

*"Winning is amazing for a minute, but then
I am striving again to reach my next goal."*

I began learning to ride when I was six, on a
little pony called Pepsi.

When I was seven, I joined my local Pony
Club – the perfect place to learn more about
riding and caring for horses.

By the time I was fourteen and riding my first
horse, Sir Barnaby, my dream of being an
event rider was starting to take shape.

Two years later, I was offered the opportunity
to train as a working pupil in Norfolk with
Ruth McMullen, the legendary riding teacher.
I jumped at the chance.

In 1987, Sir Barnaby and I won the individual gold together at the Young Rider European Championships, which was held in Poland.

Since then, hard work and determination have taken me all the way to the biggest eventing competitions in the world. I've been lucky and had success at major events like Bramham, Burghley, Badminton, Luhmühlen, Le Lion d'Angers, Hickstead, Blenheim, Windsor, Saumur, Pau, Kentucky – and the list goes on . . .

I married William Funnell in 1993. William is an international show jumper and horse breeder. He has helped me enormously with my show jumping. We live on a farm in the beautiful Surrey countryside – with lots of stables!

Every sportsman or woman's wildest dream is to be asked to represent their country at the Olympics. So in 2000, when I was chosen for the Sydney Olympics, I was delighted. It was even more special to be part of the silver medal winning team.

Then, in 2003, I became the first (and only) person to win eventing's most coveted prize – the Rolex Grand Slam. The Grand Slam (winning three of the big events in a row – Badminton, Kentucky and Burghley) is the only three-day eventing slam in the sporting world.

2004 saw another Olympics and another call-up. Team GB performed brilliantly again and won another well-deserved silver medal, and I was lucky enough to win an individual bronze.

Having had several years without any top horses, I spent my time producing youngsters, so it was great in 2010 when one of those came through – Redesigned, a handsome chestnut gelding. In June that year I won my third

Bramham International Horse Trials title on Redesigned. We even managed a clear show jumping round in the pouring rain! By the end of 2010, Redesigned was on the squad for the World Championships in Kentucky where we finished fifth.

Today, as well as a hectic competition schedule, I'm also busy training horses for the future. At the Billy Stud, I work with my husband, William, and top breeder, Donal Barnwell, to produce top-class sport horses.

And in between all that I love writing the *Tilly's Pony Tails* books, and I'm also a trustee of World Horse Welfare, a fantastic charity dedicated to giving abused and neglected horses a second chance in life. For more information, visit their website at www.worldhorsewelfare.org.

the orion star

★ ★ ★